The Narwhal
Problem

★ Also by ★

Debbie Dadey

MERMAID TALES

Coming Soon

Mermaid Tales

★Debbie Dadey★

Illustrated by
Tatevik Avakyan

BOOK 19

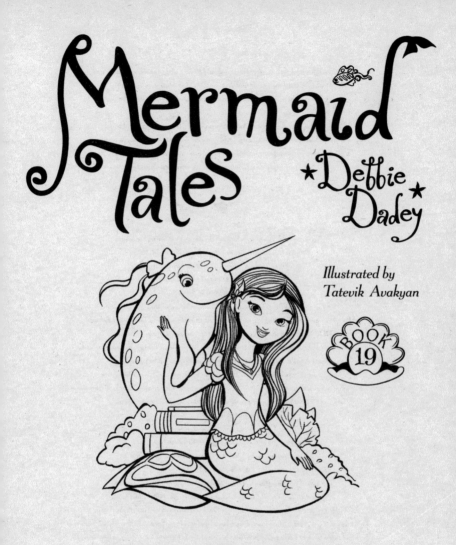

The Narwhal Problem

ALADDIN
NEW YORK   LONDON   TORONTO   SYDNEY   NEW DELHI

This book is a work of fiction. Any references to historical events, real people, or real places are used fictitiously. Other names, characters, places, and events are products of the author's imagination, and any resemblance to actual events or places or persons, living or dead, is entirely coincidental.

ALADDIN

An imprint of Simon & Schuster Children's Publishing Division

1230 Avenue of the Americas, New York, New York 10020

First Aladdin paperback edition June 2019

Text copyright © 2019 by Debbie Dadey

Illustrations copyright © 2019 by Tatevik Avakyan

Also available in an Aladdin hardcover edition.

All rights reserved, including the right of reproduction in whole or in part in any form.

ALADDIN and related logo are registered trademarks of Simon & Schuster, Inc.

For information about special discounts for bulk purchases, please contact Simon & Schuster Special Sales at 1-866-506-1949 or business@simonandschuster.com.

The Simon & Schuster Speakers Bureau can bring authors to your live event. For more information or to book an event contact the Simon & Schuster Speakers Bureau at 1-866-248-3049 or visit our website at www.simonspeakers.com.

Series designed by Karin Paprocki

Cover designed by Tiara Iandiorio

The text of this book was set in Belucian Book.

Manufactured in the United States of America 0519 OFF

2 4 6 8 10 9 7 5 3 1

The Library of Congress has cataloged the hardcover edition as follows:

Names: Dadey, Debbie, author. | Avakyan, Tatevik, 1983– illustrator.

Title: The narwhal problem / by Debbie Dadey; illustrated by Tatevik Avakyan.

Description: First Aladdin hardcover/paperback edition. | New York: Aladdin, 2019. | Series: Mermaid tales; book 19 | Summary: Kiki and her merfriends learn about coding as they compete to be the escort for a young narwhal who will visit Trident Academy with her famous parents. Includes glossary, key to the codes used, and information about safeguarding narwhals' habitats.

Identifiers: LCCN 2018040897 (print) | LCCN 2018047906 (eBook) | ISBN 9781481487160 (eBook) | ISBN 9781481487146 (pbk) | ISBN 9781481487153 (hc)

Subjects: | CYAC: Narwhal—Fiction. | Ciphers—Fiction. | Mermaids—Fiction. | Schools—Fiction.

Classification: LCC PZ7.D128 (eBook) | LCC PZ7.D128 Nar 2019 (print) | DDC [Fic]—dc23

LC record available at https://lccn.loc.gov/2018040897

For my Tennessee critique group—
Rick Starkey, Ann Starkey,
Rinda Beach, and Donna L. Martin—
thanks for all your support!

And to Huria, Ruby, Penny, and Abbie,
thanks for being mermaid fans.

Contents

1

A Special Visitor

WHAT'S SPLASHING?" Kiki Coral asked her merfriends. It was five minutes before school started, and they were floating in the large front hallway of Trident Academy. All around them merkids talked and laughed. One group

practiced walking on their hands. An angel shark glided near the carved ceiling, part of the new school security program.

Echo's dark eyes sparkled as she leaned in and whispered to Kiki and Shelly Siren, "My mom is in charge of some special visitors to our city." Echo's mother was Dr. Eleanor Reef, who ran the Conservatory for the Preservation of Sea Horses and Swordfish. Merpeople from all over the ocean came to visit it.

Kiki pushed her long black hair away from her face. "Who are they?"

Echo tugged her merfriends across the marble floor to a quiet corner.

"Have you ever heard of the Calypso family?" Echo asked.

Kiki couldn't believe her ears. "You mean the most famous scientists in the ocean are in Trident City?"

Shelly gasped. "Shelltacular! Aren't they narwhals? I've never seen one in real life."

Kiki nodded. She'd always been fascinated by pictures of narwhals and their long horns, but since they lived in cold waters, she'd never met any. Of course, Dr. Roscoe and Dr. Ethel Calypso weren't ordinary narwhals: They had written practically every book in the science section of their library! Kiki had already read at least half of them. She even owned one herself.

"Most narwhals are shy and rarely

seen by merfolk," Echo told them. "But my mother went to the Arctic University. Ethel Calypso was her roommate!"

"Do you think your mother will let us meet her old roommate?" Shelly asked.

"I can ask, but I know they are very busy," Echo said.

Kiki's heart pounded. Echo's mother was very nice. Surely she'd introduce them to her old friend. Wouldn't it be fun to meet a famous scientist?

2

Unicorns

MRS. KARP PEERED OVER her half-glasses at her third-grade class. "This will be a fun week. Tomorrow we'll start learning about codes, and a whale will visit our class in a couple days."

"We already saw a whole bunch of

humpback whales on our ocean trip," Rocky Ridge called out.

"How in the ocean will a whale fit in our classroom?" Wanda Slug shrieked. "We'll be squished to pieces!"

"I am talking about a young narwhal," Mrs. Karp told her merstudents. "Narwhals are about as tall as me when they are young. The narwhal's parents are very busy working at the conservatory and we won't be able to meet them."

"Is that the Calypso family?" Echo asked.

Mrs. Karp nodded as Shelly raised her hand. "But Mrs. Karp, I thought narwhals were porpoises."

Mrs. Karp smiled. "Actually, we're both

right. Porpoises are a kind of whale."

"Don't narwhals have those adorable horns?" Pearl Swamp asked.

"Well, it looks like a horn or tusk, but it's really a very long tooth," Mrs. Karp explained.

"A tooth!" Pearl squealed. "That's kind of icky."

Mrs. Karp shook her head. "Nature is not icky. Everything has a purpose, even if we don't understand it. Does anyone know the narwhal's nickname?"

"*Pinocchio* the Pointy Porpoise!" Rocky yelled out.

Mrs. Karp gave Rocky a stern look. "Narwhals are sometimes called the uni-corns of the sea. A unicorn is a magical horselike creature with a single horn. They are often talked about in human legends."

"So does that mean that narwhals are magical?" Echo asked.

"Of course not," Mrs. Karp said, "but many years ago they were hunted by humans for their horns. People thought they might have special powers."

Several merkids gasped. Rocky raised his hand. "What is the prettiest side of a narwhal?"

"Rocky," Mrs. Karp warned.

"The outside!" Rocky laughed, and a

few merkids giggled. Mrs. Karp smiled.

Pearl raised her hand. "Mrs. Karp, can I be the visitor's buddy?"

"What a lovely idea," Mrs. Karp said. "Narwhals are often shy, so a buddy would be helpful."

"Why Pearl?" Rocky asked. "She always gets picked to do stuff." Several other mer-students nodded in agreement.

Pearl frowned and twisted her pearl necklace in her right hand. "It was my idea!"

Mrs. Karp tapped her white tail to her chin. "I know how we can combine our lessons and select who will be our visitor's buddy. We will have a code contest!"

Kiki raised her hand. "What's a code?"

"It is a secret way of writing. Almost like a puzzle," Mrs. Karp explained. "The first student to break the code can be the narwhal's buddy."

"I'm going to do it!" Rocky bragged.

Pearl shook her head. "Nope, you don't stand a chance against me. I'm great at puzzles."

"Dr. Bottom has volunteered to help us learn about codes tomorrow. He is quite the expert," Mrs. Karp said.

When her teacher began a spelling lesson, Kiki kept thinking about the contest. How she wished she could win and be the narwhal's buddy!

Best Merfriends Ever

I WANT TO WIN," SHELLY TOLD KIKI and Echo. They were sitting at their favorite table in the corner of the school cafeteria.

"We *all* want to win," Echo said, glancing around the lunchroom. Pearl swished past them without even a glance in their

direction. Rocky was having a warty-frogfish-eating contest at his table of mer-boys.

"It would be totally wavy," Kiki agreed. In fact, she couldn't think of anything she'd like better.

"Grandfather Siren taught me a human code once," Shelly told them. "It was full of funny symbols. He said that people often put things in a secret language to keep information from their enemies."

"Do humans have a lot of enemies?" Kiki asked.

Shelly shrugged before slurping down a candy-stripe flatworm. "I guess so. I've heard they have trouble getting along sometimes. They even have wars where they fight one another!"

Kiki shivered. That sounded terrible.

"I know about codes too," Echo told them. "Last month's *MerStyle* magazine had a whole page about human spies, top secret plans, and ciphers."

"What in the ocean is a cipher?" Shelly scrunched her nose.

"It's just another word for a code," Echo explained.

Kiki stared at her shell full of ribbon worms. Suddenly she wasn't hungry at all. Everyone else already understood more about ciphers than she did. Kiki had never even seen one. What chance did she have of winning?

"I wish I knew about codes," Kiki told her merfriends. She had learned many languages from her parents, but why hadn't they or one of her seventeen brothers taught her about secret codes?

Shelly smiled. "I know what we can do. Let's finish our lunch and go the library. I bet we'll learn everything we need there!"

"Splashing good!" Echo agreed. Kiki nodded and quickly finished her ribbon worms. She was lucky to have such good merfriends. Together they would figure out how to win the contest!

Secret

I'M SORRY," MISS SCYLLA TOLD THEM. "We have one book on codes, but it's already checked out. It should be back next week."

"Thank you," Echo said. "But we need it today."

Kiki sighed. They had hit a dead end. What could they do now?

"You might check the public library," Miss Scylla suggested. "They have a lot more books."

"Thanks!" Shelly said. "We'll go after school."

After the last conch sounded, the three mergirls swam through MerPark toward the public library. They stopped to watch a pod of bottlenose dolphins dancing in the park. The merfriends were quiet as they passed the marble pillars into the oldest library in the ocean.

Kiki had been to the Trident City Library before, but she was still amazed by the pink marble walls and the sparkling diamonds in the ceiling. Thousands of rock and seaweed books filled the shelves. "Surely there's something about codes here," Kiki said.

"Shhh!" Lillian, the librarian, hissed from behind a massive granite counter.

"Sorry," Kiki whispered. "We are looking for books on codes."

"And ciphers," Echo added.

"And secret languages," Shelly said.

Lillian frowned. "I know what codes are, but you're too late. Your pal beat you to them."

They turned to see a stack of books moving toward them. Only a gold tail could be seen below the pile. "Pearl?" Shelly asked. "Did you check out all the books on codes?"

"That's not fair!" Echo put her hands on her pink hips.

Pearl peeked around her books. "I was here first. Besides, there's a few heavy ones left on a table."

"Thanks a lot," Echo grumbled.

"Come on," Kiki said, pulling her merfriends toward a long library table. Luckily, three fat books waited for them.

"Mine is called *Fun with Codes*," Echo said. "It doesn't look very fun to me."

"The study of codes is called cryptology. This book says that you can even have numbers stand for letters!" Shelly continued thumbing through *Cryptology for Beginners*.

Kiki looked up from *Ciphers in the Sea*. "This says sometimes you need a key to be able to figure out a cipher. How can we possibly know the key?"

Shelly pulled a clean piece of kelp from her school bag. "Why don't we just try some?"

"Sure," Kiki said without much hope.

"Here's an easy one. The bottom is the code. The top is what it stands for." Shelly wrote the ABCs. Below each letter she put another letter, only she started with the letter *B*.

A	B	C	D	E	F	G	H	I
B	C	D	E	F	G	H	I	J

J	K	L	M	N	O	P	Q	R
K	L	M	N	O	P	Q	R	S

S	T	U	V	W	X	Y	Z
T	U	V	W	X	Y	Z	A

"So if there is a *B*, it's actually an *A*?" Echo asked, rubbing her forehead. "This is very confusing."

"Don't worry, we'll figure it out together," Kiki said.

"Whoa," Rocky said, suddenly floating

by their table. "Did you get the last of the code books?"

Echo's face turned red. "Sorry, you can borrow this one tomorrow if you want."

"That's all right. I already have a book from school. Wait, are you studying together?" he asked.

"Of course," Shelly told him.

"You guys are crazy." Rocky shook his head. "This is a contest. You should work alone."

Kiki looked at her merfriends. They did everything together. Shouldn't they help one another now?

"Maybe Rocky is right," Echo said. "It is a competition."

"Of course I'm right," Rocky bragged as

he floated away. "We should each do what-ever it takes to win."

Shelly shrugged. "I think I'll go home and make up a code book of my own to study."

"Me too," Echo said. "We should keep what we find out a secret."

"But what about helping one another?" Kiki asked. After all, she'd helped Echo with her spelling and an art project. And she'd helped Shelly make food for a royal tea. Wouldn't they help her today?

Echo shook her head. "Nope, I really want to be the narwhal's buddy."

"Me too!" Shelly said. "I guess this is a code war!"

Kiki frowned as Shelly and Echo

swam toward the checkout desk.

Kiki would have to learn about codes without any help. She never thought she'd be in a war with her best merfriends!

5

Trouble

IS SOMETHING WRONG?" MRS. KARP asked the next morning. Her entire class was hunched over notebooks and pieces of kelp. "I've never seen you so quiet before the conch sounds."

Kiki raised her hand. "Everyone is studying their codes."

Pearl splashed up from her desk. "Rocky was peeking at my cryptology notes!"

"I did no such thing!" Rocky snapped. "I don't know what crypto-whatever is, but I didn't do it."

"This is a code catastrophe," Pearl complained. "Why does the contest have to be so hard?"

"That is quite enough!" Mrs. Karp shook her head. "This was supposed to be a fun activity. And don't worry, this afternoon Dr. Bottom and I will tell you everything you need to know about codes for the contest."

"But everyone wants to win and be the narwhal's buddy," Echo added.

Mrs. Karp glanced around. "I hope you

students know there are more important things than winning. Now, I don't want to see another code until our lesson this afternoon, unless you don't wish to take part in the competition."

Merstudents throughout the room groaned.

"Now, let's begin our spelling lesson." Mrs. Karp folded her arms and perched on the edge of her desk.

Kiki sighed. She'd been so busy learning different types of ciphers, she had forgotten to study her spelling. She hoped Echo hadn't forgotten.

"Who remembers how to spell 'octopus'?" Mrs. Karp asked.

Rocky's hand shot into the air. He spelled it correctly, then said, "I also know how to make an octopus laugh. With ten-tickles!"

Adam and a few other merkids laughed. "Get it?" Rocky asked. "They have arms called tentacles and you can tickle them!"

Mrs. Karp raised her green eyebrows. "All right, that's enough, Rocky."

Kiki didn't hear the next spelling word because a folded slip of kelp appeared on her desk. Where had it come from? She looked around and Shelly smiled at her.

Kiki opened up the note and found a row of numbers.

19-15-18-18-25

At the very bottom was a key that said A=1. Her heart pounded. It was a secret message! But could she solve it? She pulled a new piece of kelp from her notebook and drew a chart, just like the one Shelly had made the day before. Only this time, Kiki used numbers to stand for letters.

A	B	C	D	E	F	G	H	I
1	2	3	4	5	6	7	8	9

J	K	L	M	N	O	P	Q	R
10	11	12	13	14	15	16	17	18

S	T	U	V	W	X	Y	Z
19	20	21	22	23	24	25	26

Kiki was so excited about the cipher, she forgot about everything but solving it. She quickly figured out that 19 meant *S*, 15 was *O*, 18 stood for *R*, and 25 was supposed to be *Y*. She turned to look at Shelly. Both Echo and Shelly grinned at her! They were sorry for starting a code war!

"Kiki, I'm surprised at you," Mrs. Karp called out. "Are you looking at a cipher when I asked you not to?"

Oh no! Kiki was in big trouble now!

6

Fair?

"YOU SHOULDN'T BE HERE," Pearl told Kiki that afternoon. "You can't win the contest."

Kiki's eyes watered. All day long she'd felt like crying. Mrs. Karp would never let her enter the contest now. Why hadn't she put Shelly's note away? Why had she tried to solve it during spelling? Kiki threw back her shoulders and tried to be brave. "I still want to learn."

"It doesn't matter. I'm going to win anyway." Pearl sniffed the water and drifted to the front of the classroom, where Dr. Bottom floated beside Mrs. Karp. Dr. Bottom usually taught fourth grade, but he had once lectured their class about symbiotic relationships.

Shelly drifted beside Kiki. "Mrs. Karp, I'm the one who sent Kiki the coded message. If anyone should be punished, it should be me. I'm very sorry."

Echo patted Shelly's right shoulder. "I helped as well. We both apologize."

Now Kiki really felt like crying. She

put her hand on Shelly's other shoulder and admitted, "But I shouldn't have solved it during spelling. It was my fault and I'm sorry."

Mrs. Karp looked at Dr. Bottom, who smiled under his fluffy mustache. "IT APPEARS THESE YOUNG MERLADIES HAVE LEARNED SOMETHING!" he shouted. Kiki had forgotten how loud Dr. Bottom could be, but she was very grateful for his words.

"I agree," Mrs. Karp said. "In light of your apologies, you may all participate in the contest tomorrow. As long as you don't pass any more notes during class!"

"Thank you," the three merfriends said in unison.

At the same time, Pearl and Rocky snapped, "That's not fair!"

Mrs. Karp smoothed down her green hair. "As I mentioned, some things are more important than a contest. I consider honesty one of them. Now, let's learn about codes."

Pearl glared at Kiki. Kiki was happy that Mrs. Karp had given her a second chance, but was it fair?

The Contest!

THE NEXT MORNING KIKI could barely eat her lugworm cereal. Would she be able to solve the puzzle and be the narwhal's buddy? If she did, would it be fair? After all, she had worked on a cipher when she shouldn't have.

Kiki arrived ten minutes early for class and every merkid was already there! Judging from the excited chatter, they were thrilled that the contest day had finally arrived.

Mrs. Karp floated in and started their lesson. "Good morning, class. I thought we could discuss narwhals a bit more before we have our code contest. Who can tell me how narwhals sleep?"

"With their eyes closed?" Rocky called out.

"Actually, I'm not sure if they do close their eyes," Mrs. Karp said. "That is a good question for research or to ask the narwhal."

Pearl raised one hand and twisted her pearl necklace with the other. "Since narwhals need their brains to breathe, only half their brain can sleep at a time."

That didn't sound very restful to Kiki. Were narwhals always tired?

"Very good," Mrs. Karp told her, peering over her glasses. "Now, who can—"

"May I come in?" Dr. Reef said from the doorway. Lots of merstudents clapped to see her. Wanda Slug squealed and Rocky did a little dance on his brown tail. Kiki's class loved visitors. Had Dr. Reef brought the young narwhal with her? Kiki didn't see a porpoise anywhere. Maybe it was shy and hiding in the hall.

"Class, please greet Dr. Reef correctly," Mrs. Karp instructed.

The merstudents hovered beside their desks and said, "Good morning, Dr. Reef."

"Greetings to you," Dr. Reef said. "I'm glad to be here. As you may know, I work at the Conservatory for the Preservation of Sea Horses and Swordfish, but we are eager to help all ocean creatures. This week we have been working to aid narwhals."

"What's wrong with narwhals?" Shelly asked.

"Where they live is endangered," Dr. Reef explained. Kiki didn't think that sounded very good.

Dr. Reef continued, "Mrs. Karp told me about your contest, and I will take the winner to meet their narwhal buddy."

"Then let's have our contest," Mrs. Karp exclaimed.

Kiki's heart pounded as her teacher

unraveled a large piece of kelp. It was filled with a jumble of letters, and at the bottom it said *KEY WORD: UNICORNS.*

NMBHS GOMRMBOHCP

"How can a word be the key?" Rocky said, scratching his head.

"Shhh," Mrs. Karp instructed. "Now is the time to quietly put your brains to work. But don't forget what we learned in our lesson with Dr. Bottom."

Kiki sat at her rock desk with her arms folded across her tummy. Hadn't Dr. Bottom said something about a word starting a code? Then it came to her. He'd said, *Put the key word first and don't repeat any letters.*

After making a chart, Kiki worked quickly to figure out the code. The first one was pretty easy: *N* stood for *B*. She worked letter by letter until she had *BRING MERFRIENDS* on her kelp. As soon as she was finished, she put down her orange sea pen and waved her hand. Mrs. Karp glided over and looked at her answer.

A	B	C	D	E	F	G	H	I
U	N	I	C	O	R	S	A	B

J	K	L	M	N	O	P	Q	R
D	E	F	G	H	J	K	L	M

S	T	U	V	W	X	Y	Z
P	Q	T	V	W	X	Y	Z

Kiki's stomach felt funny. Had she gotten it all wrong? But when Mrs. Karp smiled, Kiki couldn't believe it. "Congratulations! We have a winner!"

"I barely got started," Rocky complained.

"No fair!" Pearl snapped. "She wasn't even supposed to be in the contest."

"Pearl, we discussed this," Mrs. Karp

said. Pearl didn't say anything else, but she frowned at Kiki.

"The answer is 'Bring merfriends,'" Dr. Reef told the class.

"What does that mean?" Kiki asked.

"It means that you get to be our narwhal visitor's buddy," Dr. Reef told them. "But you also get to meet the famous science authors with some merfriends."

Kiki's stomach did a flip!

"Oh my Neptune!" Pearl squealed. "I want to meet the famous authors." All around the classroom, merstudents muttered the same thing. As far as Kiki knew, an author had never visited Trident City before.

"I thought they were too busy," Echo said.

Dr. Reef nodded at her daughter. "They are only able to take a short break to meet the winner and a few merfriends."

Kiki couldn't believe it! She'd won the contest! And she was going to meet the authors of her favorite science books! "You mean I can really bring merfriends to meet the Calypsos?" she asked.

Dr. Reef nodded. "My friend Ethel was gracious enough to allow a few buddies to join you."

Kiki swallowed and got ready to ask a really hard question.

8

Merfriends?

BEFORE KIKI COULD SAY A word, Rocky whooshed up and threw an arm around her shoulder. "I'm your pal," he said with a grin.

"Me too!" Wanda called out.

Nearly every merstudent began chanting, "Pick me!"

"Let's give Kiki a chance to think," Mrs. Karp told the class.

Shelly touched Kiki's arm. "Don't worry, just choose a few merkids. I won't get mad."

Echo nodded. "It's all right."

Kiki could feel her face turning red. She hoped Dr. Reef would grant her request. If not, what would she do? After all, everyone wanted to meet the famous science authors. She swam beside Echo's mom and whispered, "Dr. Reef, may I take the entire class?"

"What did she say?" Pearl asked. The merkids quickly quieted down.

"This is quite a surprise," Dr. Reef said. "But if everyone agrees to be very calm, I believe it can be arranged for the whole group to go. Remember, narwhals do not like loud noises."

Everyone looked at Rocky. He shrugged. "I can be calm."

"Well then, congratulations. Let's go to the conservatory!" Dr. Reef drifted out of the classroom with twenty very excited merstudents and one teacher following behind.

Echo tapped Kiki's arm. "Thank you for taking the class," she whispered.

Kiki smiled. "It was only fair."

"I'm so excited, I think I might throw up," Wanda cried as they floated through MerPark. "We're going to meet the most famous scientists in the ocean!"

"Do you think they'll autograph my

book?" Rocky asked. He held up a book on codes written by the Calypsos.

Kiki nodded, wishing she'd thought to bring her book for them to sign. She was so excited, she could hardly think!

Mrs. Karp paused at the entrance to Trident City Plaza Hotel. "Let's remember to be calm and on our best behavior."

Rocky didn't cheer or yell out a joke. Kiki was proud of him for remaining calm. She hoped she could! After all, what if the young narwhal didn't like her?

The class silently glided over the marble floor of the Trident City Plaza Hotel.

The conservatory was housed inside the hotel. Dr. Reef waited for the merclass to gather at the shark statue outside the conservatory door.

Pearl giggled nervously. "I used to think that shark was real."

"Shhh," Mrs. Karp said. "Remember that narwhals are shy."

The merstudents nodded and swam into the conservatory. They couldn't believe what they saw.

9

Nadine, Roscoe, and Ethel

TWO ENORMOUS NARWHALS and a smaller one nearly filled the large main conservatory room. Behind her Echo squeaked, but the rest of the class was surprisingly quiet.

"Trident Academy third graders, I'd like to introduce you to our guests," Echo's mom said. "First, this is Nadine. Kiki is to be her classroom buddy for a few days."

"Good morning, Nadine," the class said softly. Pearl did a lovely curtsy and Rocky bowed. Kiki waved at Nadine and tried not to worry.

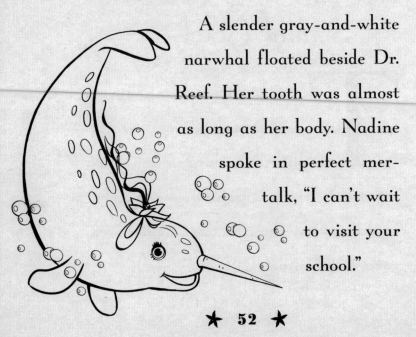

A slender gray-and-white narwhal floated beside Dr. Reef. Her tooth was almost as long as her body. Nadine spoke in perfect mer-talk, "I can't wait to visit your school."

"Class," Dr. Reef continued, "this is Dr. Ethel and Dr. Roscoe Calypso, Nadine's parents."

Mrs. Karp nodded and the merstudents said, "Good morning, Dr. Ethel and Dr. Roscoe."

Ethel smiled. "It is nice to meet you. We're surprised that there are so many of you."

Dr. Reef's face turned red. "I apologize. Our contest winner's request was to bring her entire class."

Kiki held her breath. Would the Calypso family be mad? Instead Dr. Roscoe laughed. "Kiki must be a very nice person."

Kiki grinned. A famous scientist actually said she was nice!

"Let's float over to the auditorium, where we'll have a short question-and-answer session," Dr. Reef told them.

Kiki couldn't believe she was so close to three narwhals, and two of them were famous! They were each so different. Dr. Roscoe was almost solid white with a long spiral tooth, while Dr. Ethel was a very pale gray without a tooth in sight.

Rocky drifted over to Nadine. "I thought only boy narwhals had long teeth."

Nadine giggled. "A few girls have them too. Does that surprise you?"

Rocky nodded. "I read in a library book that girls don't have them."

"It is important to read more than one book or article," Dr. Ethel said. "And to think of who wrote it and when. Do they know what they are talking about?"

Rocky stuck out his chest. "Maybe I should write a new book about narwhals."

"That would be great!" Dr. Roscoe agreed. "Perhaps it could help us with our big problem."

"What problem?" Kiki asked.

But Mrs. Karp clapped her hands for them to move into the auditorium before Roscoe could answer. The narwhals' problem was a mystery!

Problem

AS SOON AS ALL THE MER-
students were seated in the
auditorium, Pearl asked,
"Do baby narwhals have big teeth?"

Dr. Ethel smiled. "I can answer that
one. Calves are born without their long
tooth, but it starts growing during their

first year. Not all calves get a long tooth, though."

Kiki raised her hand to ask about the problem, but Mrs. Karp called on Shelly instead. "What is your long tooth used for?" Shelly asked.

"Ha-ha." Dr. Roscoe laughed. "I knew someone would ask that."

"Is it for breaking ice?" Wanda asked.

Rocky waved his right arm like a sword. "I bet it's for fighting."

"Perhaps I should leave it as a mystery," Dr. Roscoe teased.

Nadine smiled at her father. "It's hard to explain, but it has to do with showing who is in charge."

"Could you tell us what problem

brought you to Trident City?" Kiki asked. She hoped it wasn't something serious. But from the look on Dr. Reef's face, it was.

Nadine stopped smiling. "We came for help with ways to keep humans from using their land machines so much. My parents found that they are causing the ice in our home to melt."

"We hope to discover how to keep their ships away as well," Dr. Ethel added. "So many are in our waters that we've nearly run out of space to live."

Dr. Roscoe frowned. "The fishy thing is that some of the ships bring people to look at us!"

"So the very ships that want to see you

are actually hurting you?" Echo shook her head.

Dr. Roscoe nodded. "That's right."

Kiki felt guilty. She had wanted to see the narwhals just like the humans. Was there anything she could do to help?

No More Codes

"ALL RIGHT, MERSTUDENTS," Mrs. Karp announced. "It's time to swim back to school. Kiki, you'll be escorting Nadine."

Kiki smiled at the young narwhal, who tilted her long tooth in a little salute. As

they floated, Kiki tried to think of something to say to Nadine.

"I'm from the Eastern Oceans," she told
Nadine.

"That's a long way from here," Nadine
said. "Don't you miss your parents?"

Kiki nodded. "I do, but I have a lot of good merfriends at Trident Academy."

"You're lucky," Nadine said. "My parents are so busy trying to save our species, I don't get a chance to have many buddies. We travel a lot, except for winter."

Kiki wished she knew a way to help the narwhals. But what could a tiny mermaid do?

"I'm glad all that code stuff is done." Pearl sniffed the water in front of Kiki and twisted her pearl necklace. "It was making my brain hurt."

"I thought it was totally wavy," Shelly said as she splashed along beside Kiki.

"It would have been fun if I'd won," Pearl snapped. Kiki was a bit embarrassed. What would Nadine think of Pearl's grouchiness?

Nadine giggled. "I've never been a prize before."

Echo swam up beside Nadine as they moved through MerPark. "I hope you don't mind that we had a contest. Everyone wanted to be your buddy."

Nadine shook her head, and her long tooth waved through the water. "No, I think it's kind of cool."

Mrs. Karp watched as her merstudents entered Trident Academy's front hallway. "Kiki, you may show Nadine around the school now."

Pearl rolled her eyes. "Not fair."

When they were alone in the hallway,

Nadine peered at Kiki. "I was afraid to meet you by myself."

"Afraid of me?" Kiki gasped. "I was scared you wouldn't like me!"

Kiki and Nadine giggled as they went into the school library. "See that wall of books?" Kiki said. "All those were written by your parents. It must be amazing to have such a famous family."

Nadine shrugged. "I guess. Although sometimes I wonder what it would be like to be able to stay in one place all the time and make good buddies."

Kiki tapped Nadine on her shoulder. "But you have one good merfriend."

"I do?" Nadine asked. "Who?"

Kiki smiled. "Me!" At least, she hoped they could be pals.

Nadine giggled again. "Thanks. Maybe we can write each other."

"I'd like that," Kiki agreed.

"Did you say that you are learning codes?" Nadine asked.

"Yes, that's how I won the contest to be your buddy."

Nadine's eyes twinkled. "Maybe I'll even write you a letter in a secret code."

Kiki grinned. That sounded so exciting. She just hoped she'd be able to figure out the message!

12

The Plan

AFTER SHOWING NADINE the mergirls' dorms, the art room, the auditorium, and the lunchroom, Kiki took Nadine to the third-grade classroom. "Welcome, Nadine. You may sit by Kiki." Mrs. Karp pointed to a barrel sponge beside Kiki's desk.

"I'm nervous," Nadine whispered as she settled on the small seat. "I've never been in a classroom before."

"Don't narwhals have to go to school?" Kiki whispered back.

"Some do, but my parents teach me."

"Merkids are taught at home until third grade," Kiki explained. "This is my first year in a real school."

Before Kiki could say anything else, Mrs. Karp called on Nadine. "Would you care to tell us a bit about your home?"

Nadine's gray cheeks turned red, but she floated off her stool and spoke. "I live in the Arctic Ocean in the winter. Because of my parents' jobs, we travel during the summer. That's unusual for narwhals. I feel funny when I'm not sur-rounded by ice."

"I hope your parents find a way to help all narwhals," Shelly told her.

"Is there anything we can do?" Kiki wondered.

Nadine tapped her long tooth on Kiki's desk. "There are some things I wish humans would do."

"Maybe we could do them too," Echo said. She loved anything to do with humans.

Nadine bit her lip, and Kiki nodded to keep her talking. "Well," Nadine said softly. "You can start by cleaning up trash."

Rocky leaped out of his seat. "I can do that!"

Nadine smiled at Rocky. "You can fix things if they are broken, instead of throwing them away."

"I love that idea," Kiki said. "Is there anything else?"

"Not unless you can stop humans from using their land-and-water-polluting machines," Nadine said sadly.

"I know something we can do to help here in the ocean," Mrs. Karp added. "It won't stop human machines, but it will help in other ways. We can grow more kelp and algae."

Pearl waved her hand. "I read in *MerStyle* magazine that oxygen comes from algae. We need that to breathe underwater."

"And humans breathe it on land," Echo announced.

"Me too," Nadine told them. "I breathe air, not water. In fact, I'll need to go to the surface soon."

"Algae also makes a great face cream," Pearl said with a giggle.

"That's icky," Nadine sputtered.

"That's what I used to think about your tooth," Pearl pointed out. "But now I think it's fin-tastic!"

"I think you merkids are fin-tastic too," Nadine told them.

Kiki put her arm around Nadine. She knew she couldn't solve all Nadine's problems, but she could help with one: She could be a merfriend!

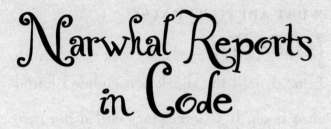

Narwhal Reports in Code

✦ ✹ ✦

(Answers are at the end.)

WHERE NARWHALS LIVE

by Shelly Siren

UIFZ MJWF JO BSDUJD XBUFST
Clue: *B* stands for *A*. I used the code
chart I made at the library.

WHAT ARE NARWHALS?

by Echo Reef

Clue: I used the shark pen cipher I found in a book. It is sometimes called pig pen, but I have no idea why. It is very tricky, but I put the key here for you. Hope you can figure it out!

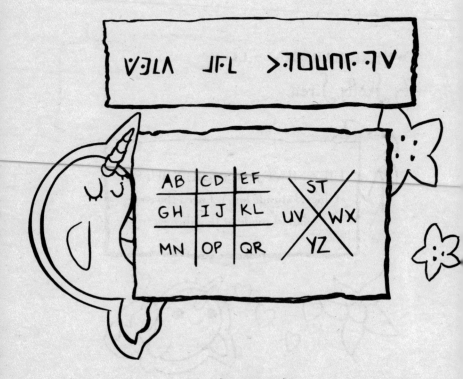

THE NARWHAL'S "PINOCCHIO" TOOTH

by Rocky Ridge

Clue: I used the cipher where numbers stand for letters. Kiki made one right before she got into trouble.

9-20   7-18-15-23-19   20-8-18-15-21-7-8
20-8-5   12-9-16

HOW ARE MALE NARWHALS DIFFERENT FROM MOST FEMALES?

by Kiki Coral

Clue: I used the code from the code contest.

QAOY AUVO JHO
FUMSO QJJQA

Answer Key

Shelly's report decoded:
They live in Arctic waters.

Echo's report decoded:
They are unicorns.

Rocky's report decoded:
It grows through the lip.

Kiki's report decoded:
They have one large tooth.

The Mermaid Song Tales

REFRAIN:

Let the water roar

Deep down we're swimming along

Twirling, swirling, singing the mermaid song.

VERSE 1:

Shelly flips her tail

Racing, diving, chasing a whale

Twirling, swirling, singing the mermaid song.

★ 78 ★

VERSE 2:

Pearl likes to shine

Oh my Neptune, she looks so fine

Twirling, swirling, singing the mermaid song.

VERSE 3:

Shining Echo flips her tail

Backward and forward without fail

Twirling, swirling, singing the mermaid song.

VERSE 4:

Amazing Kiki

Far from home and floating so free

Twirling, swirling, singing the mermaid song.

Author's Note

I BECAME INTERESTED IN CODES when I learned that Cherokee and Choctaw Indians helped pass secret messages during World War I. Because only they knew their language, it was a cipher that none of our enemies could figure out. In World War II, Navajo Indians were recruited by marines to pass messages. They became known as code talkers.

The narwhal's large tooth, like a code, is a mystery. People once believed that it was used to find food. Males often rub their tusks together in a move called tusking. This has led scientists to determine that the tooth, or tusk, is similar to a lion's mane or a peacock's feathers. It allows narwhals to compete with one another in a nonviolent way.

Sadly, the narwhals' problem isn't made up. Like polar bears, the narwhal's habitat is threatened by the Earth's warming. Let's do what we can to help the narwhal by using our cars only when necessary and walking when we can! If you want to be like our merfriends, remember the three keys to helping our planet: recycling, reusing, and restoring.

Glossary

ALGAE: There are seven thousand different types of algae, including seaweeds and pond scum. Algae produces up to 80 percent of the Earth's oxygen through photosynthesis.

ANGEL SHARK: The Pacific angel shark looks like a cross between a flattened shark and a ray. It is an endangered species.

BARREL SPONGE: The barrel sponge grows large enough that a person could actually fit inside!

BOTTLENOSE DOLPHIN: Dolphins and porpoises are often confused with each other. Porpoises are usually smaller than dolphins. The playful bottlenose dolphin's color varies from light blue to gray, with a paler underside.

CANDY-STRIPE FLATWORM: This cream-colored flatworm has red stripes and lives in rocky areas of the ocean.

CORAL: This animal lives in groups. They fix themselves to the ocean floor and make skeletons for support. One touch from a human can damage them!

HUMPBACK WHALE: The humpback whale's song can be heard miles away by other humpbacks.

KELP: Kelp is brown seaweed.

LUGWORM: You may never see a lugworm, but you might see what it left behind! Many European beaches are filled with coils of sand made by lugworms.

NARWHAL: Narwhals are a type of porpoise, mostly known for having a long, unicorn-like tooth.

OCTOPUS: The Dumbo octopus eats worms and snails. Its earlike fins give it a cartoonish look.

ORANGE SEA PEN: This creature lives in sand and mud. It resembles an old-fashioned quill pen (a sharpened feather used to write).

PORPOISE: The harbor porpoise often lives in the shallow waters of harbors and bays. While it can dive more than six hundred feet down, it must come to the surface to breathe.

RIBBON WORM: Most ribbon worms live under rocks in the sea. Some grow to be 160 feet long. That's almost the height of the Cinderella Castle at Walt Disney World!

SEA HORSE: Sea horses have rigid bodies made up of bony plates. Their heads resemble a horse's. The pygmy sea horse only grows to be one inch long!

SEAWEED: Seaweed floats freely in the ocean and can make its own food through photosynthesis.

SWORDFISH: This fast-moving fish has a long, flat bill with a swordlike appearance.

SYMBIOTIC RELATIONSHIPS: Sometimes two different organisms will interact in a long-term way. This relationship can be harmful or helpful.

WARTY FROGFISH: This fish looks like it is covered with warts! It is also called the clown frogfish.

Acknowledgments

Thanks to Kristin Laidre for helping with my narwhal research. Dr. Kristin Laidre is a principal scientist at the Polar Science Center at the Applied Physics Laboratory at the University of Washington. Any mistakes are my own.

Sending a huge hug to Tatevik Avakyan for her fabulous illustrations. She has outdone herself with this incredible cover. Thanks also for the amazing work of designers Karin Paprocki and Tiara Iandiorio. For keen eyes and dedication to making things right, thanks to copy editor Valerie Shea and production editor Rebecca Vitkus.

Pearl Swamp is going to be the Winter Princess at this year's festival, but will her parents' surprise spoil her big day?

Winter Princess

PEARL SWAMP COULDN'T believe her luck. Out of all the third graders at Trident Academy, her name had been drawn to be the princess at this year's Winter Festival! If it had been a merboy, they would have had a winter prince. Every year Trident City celebrated the end of the coldest waters with a huge party at the People Museum. All the money raised went to help families in need.

Pearl had dreamed all her life of being the winter princess! It was the most exciting thing to ever happen to her. She would wear a fancy dress, give the welcome speech, and be the official ambassador for her school. She couldn't wait to share the news with her parents.

Pearl zipped through MerPark, around a glass squid, and dashed inside the large pink shell she shared with her parents. "Mom!"

Her mother popped out of her home office and smiled. "Pearl! I've been waiting for you."

"I have great news," they both said at the same time.

Pearl was surprised. Did her mother already know?

"What's your news?" her mother asked.

"You can go first," Pearl said.

Her mother clapped her hands. "You are not going to believe it! You're getting a baby brother!"

Pearl hadn't expected that at all. She opened her mouth. She closed her mouth. Finally, she squeaked, "A baby?"

"Yes," squealed her mother. "Isn't it exciting? We're adopting a little boy."

"A boy?" Pearl muttered. "Why a boy?"

Mrs. Swamp giggled like a young child. "Well, we already have a lovely daughter.

Don't you think a boy will be nice?"

Pearl frowned. A baby girl might have been fun. She could have dressed it in frilly dresses and had tea parties. But she wasn't so sure about a boy.

"Does Daddy know about this?"

Her mother smiled. "Well, of course. This is something we've planned for a long time."

Her parents had talked to her about adopting a baby, but that had been a while ago. Pearl thought they had forgotten about the whole thing. Why in the ocean did they want a baby? Wasn't she enough for them?

"Pearl?"

Pearl wanted to stomp her gold fins and

tell her parents to forget about a baby. But her mother looked so hopeful and happy, Pearl just couldn't. Instead she fibbed, "I can't wait."

Her mother gave her a hug. "I've dreamed of giving our new baby a good home. Our family will be complete."

Pearl thought it had been pretty perfect with just the three of them, but she didn't say so. "Oh, that reminds me," her mother said. "I'm going to clean out the craft room for the baby's bedroom."

"What?" Pearl couldn't believe her ears. Pearl and her mother loved their hobby room. It was filled with colorful shells, beads, and even ribbons. They'd had many fin-tastic times making all sorts of fun creations. And now her mom was just going to get rid of it all? "But where will we do our projects?"

"Don't worry," Mrs. Swamp said. "Most merpeople don't have a craft room and they do just fine."

Pearl frowned. Losing her craft room did not sound fine at all.

Mrs. Swamp floated up their curving marble staircase. She disappeared around the corner before Pearl realized her mother had forgotten to ask about Pearl's good news!

Looking for another great book?
Find it
IN THE MIDDLE.

Fun, fantastic books for kids
in the in-be**TWEEN** age.

IntheMiddleBooks.com

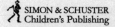